The Case of the

ROBBED RECIPE

COLLAR CASES 1

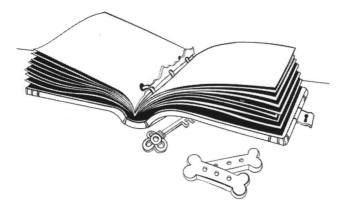

written by
Amanda Trumpower

illustrations & cover by Sarah Johnson

Knotted
Oak
PRESS

Paperback ISBN: 978-1-939586-11-7

Summary: Investigative journalists Mittens Meow and Alex Digger hurry to the rescue when Alex's favorite baker discovers a shocking theft which threatens the future of her business. Can Mittens and Alex uncover the culprit in time?

———

supplemental materials to the author (amanda@jtrumpower.com) for potential display on Collar Cases.com.

Student artists of any age are encouraged to use Collar Cases characters in their own art. They may post online, provided no profit is made and the author & illustrator of the source material are appropriately credited (Amanda Trumpower, Sarah Johnson).

Students are encouraged to submit any fanart to the author for display on Collar Cases.com.

Visit www.AmandaTrumpower.com for more information.

Scriptures: *Holy Bible*, New Living Translation, copyright © 1996, 2004, 2015 by Tyndale House Foundation. Used by permission of Tyndale House Publishers, Inc., Carol Stream, Illinois 60188. All rights reserved.

To Mom & Dad, my encouragers from the beginning. Thank you.

contents

bible theme: revenge

66 Dear friends, never take revenge. Leave that to the righteous anger of God. For the Scriptures say,
"I will take revenge;
I will pay them back,"
says the Lord.

Romans 12:19

one
bowwow goes bonkers

ON A JUNE AFTERNOON, the town of Bowwow gathered in Central Park to celebrate an important day. Among those gathered were the *Bowwow Bark*'s top investigative reporters, Mittens M. Meow and her partner, Alex D. Digger.

Alex turned a page in his newspaper. He bought it on the way to the park because he wanted to read the comics. Now, the inside story caught his attention.

He elbowed Mittens. "Did you see this report? 'Three houses targeted last night in graffiti prank.' What a shame."

He read the next line and frowned. "My goodness! Grandma Basset was one of the victims. Did she say anything about it to you?"

Mittens stood on tiptoe, trying to see the stage better. "That's nice, Alex."

For the last seventy years, Grandma Basset had made delicious treats for cats and dogs of all ages at her Tasty Treats factory. Today, she was about to unveil her

200th dog biscuit flavor. Every dog in town was dying to know the secret.

"Looks like the other graffiti victims were Mayor Nut and Dr. Honda." Alex continued reading. "Police found the word *soon* sprayed across their garage doors. Now that's a funny thing to put on a garage door."

"Uh-huh," Mittens said.

Alex folded the paper up. "This sounds like a real mystery. What do you think?"

In front of him, a fox turned around. She pressed a claw to her lips.

"I'll read it later," Mittens said. "The ceremony is starting."

Alex sighed.

In Alex's opinion, Mittens was the toughest reporter at the *Bowwow Bark*. She could turn a bulldog bodyguard into a cowering poodle with a single glare.

And she was smart. When she investigated a story, she didn't stop digging until she found the truth...even if that meant facing a little danger.

Privately, Alex wondered if Mittens enjoyed danger a little too much. As for him, his life was simple. He lived by three rules:

1) Never say no to Mittens.

2) Never underestimate the power of a smile.

3) Never leave Mittens in charge of snacks.

There was also Rule #3.5: "Submit articles relatively on time," but he didn't worry about that too much. Their editor was used to receiving Alex's work late.

Usually with food stains.

On stage, Mayor Nut tapped the microphone. Grandma Basset was up there too, sitting on a folding chair off to the side.

"Quiet, please." Mayor Nut said. "Grandma Basset would like to begin."

It took Grandma Basset three whole minutes to shuffle from the chair to the microphone. Mittens drummed her pen against her notepad.

Patience was not her foremost quality.

"Walks kinda slow, doesn't she?" Alex whispered. "Maybe she needs to eat some of her Chili Pepper & Bacon treats! Those always put extra fire in my step. But I tell you what, the gas afterwards is—"

The fox shushed him again.

Alex made a face at her.

"Welcome, ladies and gentlemen." Grandma Basset's voice warbled like bad cell signal. "Thank you for supporting Tasty Treats all these years. It is an honor to introduce your taste buds to our bicentennial flavor."

"What does bicentennial mean?" Alex whispered.

"Two hundred." Mittens answered without looking up from her notepad.

"We have worked hard to bring you this new culinary experience," Grandma Basset said. "I hope you enjoy. Mayor Nut! The recipe book, please."

Mayor Nut brought the book to her. It looked heavy. It had yellow pages edged in gold and an elaborate lock on the cover.

Grandma Basset unlocked it with a key hanging around her neck.

She peeled back the cover.

"I give you—"

She gasped.

Alex gripped his pencil. "What? What's wrong? Why did she stop?"

Mittens leaned in, ears pricked forward.

"It's gone." Grandma clutched her paws to her chest. "Someone stole the recipe!"

Alex's ears jumped into triangles. He grabbed Mittens's arm. "No! Say it isn't so!"

The crowd spoke at the same time:

"Who would do that?"

"What are we going to do?"

"What was the 200th flavor?'

"Anybody know where the bathroom is?"

Mittens put her paws on her hips. "Alex, the graffiti on the garage doors will have to wait. We just found our next story."

two
suspects and suspicions

MITTENS COULDN'T THINK with everyone shouting. She was glad when the police arrived and directed the crowd to visit the park's Ferris wheel, picnic games, and food vendors. Now, she and Alex stood on stage with Grandma Basset and Mayor Nut.

"Who could have done this?" Grandma Basset cried into a handkerchief.

"Don't worry, ma'am. We'll get to the bottom of it." Mittens flipped open her notebook. "Who had access to your recipe book?"

Grandma Basset blinked from behind her round glasses. "No one. I guard it closely. I'm the only one with the key. When I'm not using it, I lock the book up in my office safe."

"Who knows the combination?" Alex said.

"Just me."

Mittens tapped her pen against her pages. "Was anyone in your office recently?"

Grandma Basset stopped to think. "I had two meetings this morning. But my employees wouldn't do a thing like this!"

"They could have," Alex said. "If they got into your safe while it was open, they're the prime suspects. Unless the missing recipe was stolen by aliens!"

Mittens sighed. "It wasn't aliens, Alex."

"How do you know? Some aliens can walk through walls. It's a fact."

Mittens wanted to tell him there were no *facts* about aliens because there were no *aliens*. But they'd been down this road before, so she just moved on. "I need the names of the employees you met with."

Grandma Basset took off her glasses. They were streaky with tear stains. She wiped them on her sweater. "My first meeting was with Robert Roland. My second was with Dotty Dipstick."

Mittens divided her page in half with a long line. She wrote the suspects' names on each side. "What are their positions in your company?"

"Robert is the C.F.E.—Chief Flavor Engineer. Dotty led the marketing department." Grandma Basset sniffed. "Until she quit this morning."

Mittens and Alex traded a look.

"I was so surprised! I loved having her on my team." Grandma Basset put her glasses back on and blinked.

"Was she angry?" Mittens said.

Grandma Basset's ears drooped. "Yes. I'm afraid she was."

Alex flipped his notebook shut with a snap. He put his paws on his hips. "I think we should chat with Miss Dipstick."

"I think we should chat with both of them." Mittens slid her notebook into its designated space in her purse. "Grandma, I don't want to be insensitive, but couldn't you just write the recipe down again?"

Grandma Basset blushed. "I'm not as young as I used to be. I don't remember the exact measurements. But even if I did design the flavor again, it wouldn't matter. Whoever stole the recipe knows the secret. If we don't get it back—and soon—I'll have to start over!"

"I thought Mr. Roland designs the flavors," Mittens said. "Maybe he remembers."

Grandma Basset shook her head. "He designs lots of flavors, but I do the special ones. And I always keep final recipes a secret—even from my staff."

Alex sighed. "I don't get it. Sure, Mr. Roland and Miss Dipstick were in the office, but how could either of them take the recipe if the book was locked up in the safe?"

Mittens smiled at him. That was a good question. For all his talk of aliens and cheeseburgers, Alex was a great reporter.

"Did you leave the office during the meeting?" Mittens said.

Grandma Basset pressed a hand to her chest and gasped. "I did! I needed something from the records room."

"Was the safe open?"

Grandma Basset howled. "Bless my cookie sheets, it was! I was checking a few details before today's celebration and I forgot to shut the door before I left. Why have I been so forgetful lately? Yesterday, I nearly left the house in my slippers. Maybe I should close the company until I get my head back together."

Alex's eyes were huge. If it were possible, it looked like his cream fur turned even whiter.

"There, there, Grandma." Mayor Nut patted her on the shoulder. "It'll be all right."

"Yeah, don't worry!" Alex slung an arm around Mittens. "We'll find your recipe! We'll find it *today*, even. Please don't close down the factory. Give us a chance."

Mittens crossed her arms. "What's with you? You never get this excited about a new case."

Alex pulled an empty box of Tasty Treats from his backpack. "She has to keep baking. I'm all out of snacks."

three
gathering clues

"DID YOU FIND ANYTHING YET?"

Alex was in Grandma Basset's office, searching for clues with Mittens.

At least, he was *trying* to search for clues.

It was hard to concentrate with his stomach growling this loud. He wanted to stop for a hamburger on the way, but Mittens said they didn't have time.

Funny thing about Mittens. She never seemed to give food the priority it deserved. Now that Grandma Basset had threatened to shut down Tasty Treats, all he could think about was his empty treat box. And his even emptier stomach.

"No clues yet," Mittens called from Grandma Basset's desk. She opened the next drawer and leafed through the papers. "Check the perimeter. Maybe the thief left evidence on the floor."

Alex crawled across the carpet, studying each baseboard. After a few minutes, he spotted a small piece of red cloth in the corner.

"I found something!"

Mittens left the desk and joined him. "This looks like a piece of shirt. Great job, Alex! Did you find anything else?"

He looked at the carpet again. He pointed to a small French fry covered in chocolate icing. "There's that."

Mittens wrinkled her nose. "Gross! Why would Grandma Basset eat *that*?"

"Maybe it's not hers." Alex pressed the fry close to his nose. He sniffed. "I have the strangest feeling I've seen this before..."

Mittens returned to the desk. "You've seen lots of French fries, Alex."

"No, I mean this specific kind of fry."

Mittens wasn't listening, so he pocketed the fry and examined the safe. It was locked.

He slumped to the floor. "I don't want Grandma to close down the factory. What will I eat?"

"Have you considered vegetables?"

Alex made a face. "Gosh, Mittens, I'm not desperate."

They found no other clues. They turned off the office lights and left.

"You'll be fine," Mittens said as they walked down the hall. "You watch so many baking shows. You should make your own treats! You're a great cook."

Alex beamed. "Aw, thank you. And here I thought you hated my cooking."

Mittens held up a paw. "I don't like your spaghetti-flavored popcorn. Trust me, that's not unreasonable."

"Speaking of food, I'm still hungry. Can we grab a burger now?" He pressed the button to call for the elevator. "Wowza-Burger is on the way to Dotty Dipstick's house."

He smiled as his imagination filled with images of cheesy, melted goodness spreading across a steaming hamburger.

"I want to order a triple-decker bacon burger with fries. And a chocolate milkshake!"

The elevator arrived with a quiet *ding*. They stepped inside.

"All right," Mittens said. "I suppose I'm

hungry too." She pushed the button for the ground floor. "I'll get a salad."

"You are so weird."

The doors slid shut. As the mechanism slowly lowered them down, Alex breathed deeply. The elevator smelled like beef and cheese. The sauce department was only one floor above them.

"Heaven," he declared. "Simply heaven. Say, did you know aliens prefer salad over burgers? Maybe you're an alien and you don't even know it! That would be cool. I'd probably ask for your autograph."

four
dotty dipstick the dalmatian

"PLEASE DEPART!" Dotty Dipstick called from behind her front door. It was painted shades of neon orange and green that made Alex's eyes cross. "I don't speak to reporters. You are disturbing the flower power."

"Oh brother," Alex muttered.

Not to be deterred, Mittens put her paws on her hips. "Miss Dipstick, we only want to ask you a few questions. We won't disturb any of your, um, flowers."

The door opened.

A rush of perfume shot up Alex's nose, making his head seize into a knot and his eyes water. Dotty Dipstick stood a good four heads taller than him. She wore a long, flowing red dress and a headband behind her ears. Perfume rolled off her as if she were a scared skunk.

Alex wiggled his nose to fight back a sneeze.

Dotty frowned. "This can't take long. I have lemongrass cupcakes in the oven. They're organic, you know."

The thought of organic lemongrass cupcakes was enough to make Alex gag. And if that wasn't bad enough, the perfume continued to overwhelm his nose. He put a paw over his heart. He felt like he would faint.

"My goodness, Miss Dipstick!" Mittens elbowed him hard in the ribs. "You're wearing such a pretty dress. How long have you had it?"

"Ouch!" Alex grumbled as his eyes watered. "What's your problem?"

"Isn't that a nice dress Miss Dipstick has on?"

Alex shrugged. "I dunno. It's a dress. Although it's a little hard to see because my eyes are still watering—"

"Alex, it's a red dress."

"I know. I'm not colorblind." His eyes widened as he remembered the scrap of red cloth from Grandma Basset's office. "Oh!

Oh yes! It's a nice *red* dress." He winked at Mittens.

Dotty looked confused. "Is there something specific you want? My oven timer will go off any moment."

"We're helping investigate the theft of Grandma Basset's recipe," Mittens said. "I assume you've heard it's missing."

"Yes," Dotty said. "How sad."

She did not look sad to Alex.

"We understand the two of you had a meeting this morning," Mittens said. "You resigned from your position?"

"I sure did. And let me tell you, it's the best decision I've ever made. Nobody understands my artistic vision! I am done being restrained by the corporate straitjacket."

Alex didn't know what that meant, but he wrote down *corporate straitjacket* anyway. He'd ask Mittens about it later.

"Where did you go after the meeting?" Mittens said.

Dotty raised her nose into the air. "To

have breakfast at the Organic Waffle Hut with my friend, Patty Pastel. She'll confirm my story."

Alex rolled his eyes. Organic Waffle Hut, huh? That tracked.

"We had to hurry," Dotty continued, "because she was starting her shift soon at the Stephen Porcupine Art Museum. She's a tour guide, you know." Dotty gave Alex another glare. "And she *loves* my lemongrass cupcakes."

Mittens wrote the information down in her precise handwriting. Just watching all those straight *t*'s and perfectly dotted *i*'s gave Alex's paw a cramp.

"Thank you for your help, Miss Dipstick," Mittens said when she was done. "Enjoy your cupcakes."

Once they were safely in the car, Alex made gagging noises. "What some people will eat! Hey, can we stop for a snack before we talk to Robert? The restaurant we passed on the way has beef-flavored chicken nuggets with bacon sprinkles."

Mittens sighed and started her car. "Oh, Alex…"

five
robert roland
the raccoon

ON THE WAY to Robert Roland's home, Mittens drove past Central Park. She was steering around the bend when suddenly, Alex pressed a paw to the window.

"There he is!"

Mittens parked the car. They jogged up the path.

"Mr. Roland!" Mittens called. "Can we talk to you?"

He turned around. He was a pudgy raccoon, dressed in a white T-shirt and red suspender pants. He squinted. "Who are you?"

Mittens pulled out her notebook.

"Mittens Meow, reporter for the *Bowwow Bark*. This is my partner, Alex Digger. We're investigating the theft of Grandma Basset's recipe."

Roland looked at the grass. "Shocking tragedy. Such a sweet old lady. Who would do something like that?"

"We know you had a meeting with Grandma Basset yesterday." Alex leaned in close, eyes narrowed. "*And* we know her safe was unlocked. Got anything to say for yourself, buster?"

Mittens smacked her forehead. This was not how she planned to handle the interview.

Roland crossed his arms. "What are you suggesting, *puppy?*"

Mittens cleared her throat and stepped between them. "We're not suggesting anything, sir. We wondered if you saw anything suspicious."

"I certainly did not. Grandma Basset left for a few minutes to retrieve some copies from the printer. I reviewed my notes while she was gone."

"And what was the meeting about?" Alex was still trying his tough guy routine. Mittens made a mental note to discuss it with him later.

"Not that it's any of your business," Roland said, glaring, "but we were having an argument. I wanted her to use one of my creations for the 200th flavor. She wanted to use hers."

Mittens scribbled notes without looking

at her paper. "What does that mean, exactly?"

"Tasty Treats develops several new flavors every year. As her Chief Flavor Engineer, I design most of them. Grandma Basset only makes one occasionally—yet hers always receive the most attention."

Alex couldn't believe his ears. "You mean Grandma Basset doesn't create them in her mother's original kitchen? With the big mixing bowl from her great-great grandfather Silas?"

Mittens sighed. "He reads the back of all the boxes. He's a big fan." To Alex she said, "Grandma already told us Robert does a lot of the work."

"Yeah, but..." Alex looked like he'd just discovered his best friend was secretly a vegetable in disguise. "I thought she at least *started* them in her kitchen."

"That may be how Tasty Treats started, young man, but that's not how we do things anymore." He adjusted the straps of his suspenders. "Now if you'll excuse me, I have things to do."

Roland hurried away. In his haste, a piece of paper fell out of his pocket. It fluttered to the sidewalk.

Alex picked it up. "Wait a minute, Mr. Roland. You forgot—"

"Let me see that." Mittens edged closer. "It's a coupon. '50% off your next visit to the Yodeling Toad.' What in the world is a Yodeling Toad?"

Alex's eyes grew round as spaceships. "What's the Yodeling Toad? It's only the greatest pizza place in town! They have puppets and video games and a playground. Oh, and of course, they have the Yodeling Toad himself."

Mittens sighed. "I know I'm going to regret asking this, but here it goes: Who is the Yodeling Toad?"

"You've never heard of Yancy? He wears lederhosen and sings show tunes and camp songs on stage. And he yodels. Talk about high-class entertainment!"

"The things I do for this job." Mittens turned the coupon over and read the fine print. "The restaurant doesn't open until dinner. Let's type up our notes at my place. When it's time, we'll put on our sneaky clothes and follow Mr. Roland."

"Excellent." Alex rubbed his paws together. "It's time for my pre-dinner snack."

six
the yodeling toad

MITTENS POURED herself a glass of milk and walked to her desk in the living room. Alex slouched on the couch. His paw dangled in a bowl of popcorn as he watched the chef on screen take something out of the oven.

"What are you watching?" Mittens said.

"*Cool Calvin's Cake Confectionary*. He decorates amazing birthday cakes from his crazy bakery in New York. In this episode, he's making the blue spaceship of a time-traveling alien." He swallowed some popcorn. "How are our notes coming?"

Mittens narrowed her eyes as she took a

seat behind her laptop. "*Our* notes are coming along great. Thanks for asking. Will you be contributing anything?"

Alex tapped his temples. "It's all up here, Mittens. Trust the process."

Mittens couldn't think of anything to say to that, so she went back to work. After half an hour, she closed her laptop.

"I'm finished. Let's get changed into our sneaky clothes and get over to the Yodeling Toad. We want enough time to find a hiding spot before Roland arrives."

Alex looked at his watch. "We still have plenty of time before the restaurant opens. Can't we watch the rest of this episode?"

Mittens was eager to crack the case, but one look at Alex's puppy eyes melted her resolve like a gooey chocolate chip cookie.

She set down her glass of milk and squeezed next to him on the couch. "Only if I get to watch it with you."

"Awesome! You want some popcorn? I only sneezed on half of it."

A little while later, Mittens found herself sitting on a pile of pine cones. They were hiding in the shrubs around the Yodeling Toad parking lot. Although her black long-sleeved shirt covered her arms, she felt a breeze against her whiskers. She shivered.

"How long are we going to sit in the bushes?" Alex said. "My paws are cold."

Mittens pushed her binoculars through the branches. She scanned the parking lot. "Patience is the key element of superior investigation, Alex. Never forget it."

"But why don't we go inside now? We could get a table by the door."

"We can't do that! Someone might think I actually eat here!"

The sound of car tires crunching over gravel interrupted them.

Mittens peered through the binoculars. Next to her, Alex made two circles with his paws and pretended to look.

"What do you see?" Mittens said.

"My fur. I have hairy paws."

That was Alex for you.

Roland parked his car. He shoved his hands into his pockets, glanced over his shoulder, and headed for the entrance.

Mittens memorized his license plate. When she had it safe in her memory, she quietly counted to ten. They followed him inside.

Mittens pushed open the door and stepped into a lobby so noisy, it made her skull vibrate. A mob of kids shoved her against the wall, storming from dining tables on the right to a game room on the left.

Alex helped her up. "I forgot to warn you. Yodeling Toad patrons tend to be a little enthusiastic."

"You don't say."

At the checkout counter in front of them, a line of cash registers chimed in succession as parents bought arcade tokens for their kids. TVs blared from their perches in ceiling corners while annoyingly catchy tunes boomed through a sound system by a karaoke stage.

And everywhere she looked, Mittens saw life-sized mechanical animals. Their jaws swung open and shut with all the grace of an ancient elevator, arms karate-chopping the air sporadically.

Mittens pressed her ears to her head. *"How can you stand all this noise?"*

Alex waved a paw. "You get used to it. The checkout counter sells earplugs for parents. I could get you some if you want."

A cat waitress wearing a duck costume passed by. She carried a plate of chocolate-covered French fries. After she left, Mittens saw a flash of black-and-gray fur in the distance.

"There he is!"

They squeezed through tables as they tried to catch up with Roland. They passed a long buffet counter in the center of the room. Mittens wasn't sure, but she suspected Alex snagged a slice of pepperoni pizza as they went by.

Mittens caught a glimpse of raccoon tail off to the left. But just as quickly, she lost it again among the heads and ears of Yodeling

Toad patrons.

Mittens refused to let Roland escape. She squeezed behind a waitress in a squirrel costume and turned a corner. She nearly ran into the thick red curtain blocking her path. Alex smacked into her from behind. They fell over.

When they untangled themselves, they flattened against the wall. Mittens nudged the curtain aside.

It revealed a small back room, far quieter than the main space. This area held several round tables topped with nice tablecloths and candles. Along the back wall, more red curtains blocked off private booths.

"This is the VIP section," Alex whispered. "Nice booths. Candle lighting. Live musicians. Very hard to get into."

Roland approached a corner booth. Someone had partially drawn the curtain around the table, hiding half the booth in shadows. Roland slid onto the empty bench. He pulled the curtain shut.

"Whoooaaa," Alex whispered. "It's a conspiracy! I'll bet they're talking about aliens and the pyramids."

A light flashed behind the curtain.

Flame took to a candle wick, and then a

soft yellow light illuminated Roland's silhouette.

There was a bird shape across from him.

"Who do you think that is?" Alex said.

"I don't know," Mittens said, "but we're not leaving here until we find out."

They watched the booth for a long time. Finally, Roland slid the curtain back. He walked to the exit, a brown paper bag in his hands.

The bird remained in the shadows.

Alex sniffed. "What do you think he has in the bag? Donuts?"

"No, Alex, I don't think it's donuts."

Mittens eased the curtain open a little wider. Maybe she could sneak up to the booth and peek inside without being caught.

"I need to know who that is."

Alex pointed to the door. "But Mr. Roland is getting away! Maybe he has the recipe."

Mittens paused to think. "What if we split up?"

"What if we get hurt?"

Mittens looked at the booth. She hated to let such a juicy lead slip through her paws. The most exciting story she'd worked in months was *right there!*

But Alex was right. It was dangerous, and they had to focus on recovering the recipe for Grandma Basset.

She sighed. "Fine. Let's go."

They followed Roland from a safe distance. They rounded a corner just as a birthday party rushed by, kids high on a sugar buzz. Mittens and Alex were forced to stop until the stampede cleared away.

Roland was gone.

"We have to get out of the crowd!" Alex said.

He pulled Mittens to the side of the room. They pressed their backs against the pizza-patterned wallpaper and inched toward the door.

There was a stage a few yards ahead. It was big, with many seats lined up in front. As Mittens watched, the spotlight clicked on. A pool of white light appeared on the floor. A frog piano player in the corner of the room polished her keys with her elbow.

Mittens groaned. "Now what?"

The frog counted a silent, "One! Two! Three!" and then plunged her fingers onto the keys.

Alex clasped his paws together. "He's coming!"

"Who's coming?"

But Alex wasn't paying attention. He pushed his way to the front of the stage where a large crowd of kids gathered. Together, they clapped and barked and whistled.

"Ladies and gentlemen," said a drawly Southern male voice over the speakers, "put your paws and claws together to welcome Yancy, the Yodeling Toad!"

A toad dressed in bright green lederhosen cartwheeled onto the stage. He grabbed the microphone, opened his mouth, and let loose a yodel that sounded like a screaming billy goat on a collapsing roller coaster.

Mittens flinched. Her fur poofed instantly as if she'd touched an electrical outlet.

The toad yodeled away. Risking permanent hearing loss, Mittens pushed through the crowd until she could grab Alex's collar. She hauled him out the front door, leaving behind the customers, the costumed waitresses, and that awful yodeling toad.

When they stepped out into the quiet parking lot, Mittens inhaled deeply.

Silence. It was beautiful.

Alex pointed. "Look! Mr. Roland is getting into his car."

"Hide!" Mittens shoved him into the bushes.

Alex landed on a pine cone and howled.

Mittens shushed him. She grabbed her binoculars from their hiding place in the bush and brought the raccoon's image into focus.

He sat in his car, peering inside the paper bag. A smile spread over his face. He dropped the bag into the passenger seat.

Mittens sprang to her feet. "He's leaving. Come on!"

seven
the robber and the mastermind

MITTENS DROVE with her headlights off. They tailed Roland from a safe distance all the way back to his house. She parked around the block. They tiptoed to his driveway.

"You investigate the windows," Mittens whispered across the beam of her flashlight. "Figure out what's in the bag. I'll search his car."

Alex saluted.

He crept to the living room window. The lamps in the corner lit up the room like a fish tank. Alex hooked his paws on the window sill, stood on his tiptoes, and slowly raised his head.

He could just see over the edge. Roland sat by the coffee table, counting fat stacks of money. Alex's eyebrows climbed his forehead. He snapped a picture with his night-vision camera and ducked back into the bushes.

Meanwhile, Mittens searched the car. She rummaged through the glove compartment, the door pockets, and under the seats. She couldn't find anything more suspicious than an old fast-food cup.

She shoved her head deep under the driver's seat. She felt something crinkle under her paws.

Finally! A clue!

She sat in the driver's seat and pointed her flashlight down. The paper was a letter. It was addressed to Roland. It thanked him for his good work stealing the recipe. The instructions for tonight's meeting at the Yodeling Toad were written on the back.

The letter was signed...

"Ruffled Feathers? Who in the world is Ruffled Feathers?"

Alex's head appeared outside the car window.

Mittens screamed and dropped her flashlight.

"Shhh!" Alex waved his paws. "Do you want him to hear us? Check it out. I got a picture of him counting stacks of money. Lots of money! What did you find?"

"A letter that proves Mr. Roland was hired to steal the recipe. It's signed by some guy named Ruffled Feathers."

"What do we do now?"

Mittens took her phone out of her pocket. "We call the sheriff."

Twenty minutes later, Sheriff Doberman led Roland out of the house in handcuffs. The bubble on top of the squad car pulsed red and blue in the driveway. Mittens noticed Alex locked in a hypnotic stare with the flashing light. She pulled him away when he started to drool.

Sheriff Doberman paused on the sidewalk so they could talk to the raccoon.

"Who is Ruffled Feathers, sir?" Mittens asked, pen poised above her notebook. "Who hired you to do this?"

"More importantly, why did you do it?" Alex said. "What would the world have done without Grandma Basset's treats? I nearly starved to death trying to solve this case."

Mittens cleared her throat. "You can answer my question first, sir."

"I'm not telling you anything," Roland said. "I know my rights! The right to bear arms. The right to free speech. The right for women to vote—"

"I think you're looking for 'the right to have an attorney,'" Alex said.

"That's the one. I want my lawyer!"

Alex wielded his best puppy eyes. "Could you at least tell us where you put the recipe?"

But Roland only pushed his whiskered

nose in the air. The officers led him away into the squad car.

Alex's tail sagged to the floor. "We're back where we started."

Mittens patted his arm. "Don't worry, pal. I have an idea."

———

The next morning, the entire town assembled for the second time in Central Park. Grandma Basset and Mayor Nut stood on the stage again. Mittens and Alex squeezed to the front of the crowd.

Alex elbowed his partner and pointed. Robert Roland stood a few rows down, accompanied by a police officer.

"Everyone," Grandma Basset said into the microphone, "thank you for your patience during these stressful days. I also want to thank Miss Meow and Mr. Digger for their wonderful work finding the recipe thief."

The crowd offered a round of polite

applause. Mittens and Alex traded high fives.

"Now, as for the matter of the missing flavor…" Grandma Basset sighed. "I regret to inform you the recipe is lost forever."

The crowd gasped.

Alex seized his heart and fell over in a stiff-legged faint.

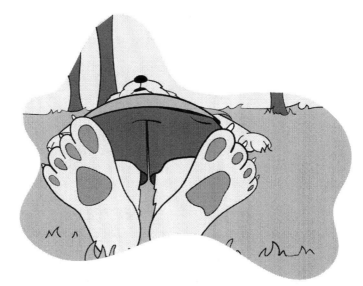

Grandma Basset waited for Mittens to revive him before she continued. "Don't worry, Alex. I have good news too."

The crowd laughed.

"Instead of my original recipe, it's time to celebrate the talents of new chefs. To that end, I'm pleased to announce Mr. Roland's Bacon Serenity will be our bicentennial flavor."

The crowd went wild. Some of the dogs drooled. Alex fainted again.

Robert took a step forward. The surprise was written all over his face. "Do...do you mean it?"

Grandma Basset nodded. "Sheriff Doberman told me you're sorry. You still owe community service, but your creative talents will get the recognition they deserve."

Tears welled up in Roland's eyes.

"Oh, thank you—thank you! I'm so sorry for what I did. It was wrong. I should have talked to you instead of following those horrible instructions from Ruffled Feathers."

Mittens saw her moment and she seized it. "How did you hear about Ruffled Feathers, sir? Did he approach you? Or did you approach him?"

Roland shrugged. "I got a letter in the mail one day, asking if I wanted to get back at Grandma Basset for sidelining my work."

"Do you still have this letter?"

Roland agreed to send it to Mittens first thing in the morning.

With the mystery solved and the new flavor announced, Mayor Nut delivered a speech to wrap up the festivities. The band played a song. The crowd moved on to enjoy the carnival games and the food booths— Alex played Bobbing for Chicken Legs at least nine times—but Mittens couldn't relax.

Who was Ruffled Feathers?

Later that afternoon, Mittens and Alex typed up their story in front of Alex's TV.

Or rather, Mittens typed up their story while Alex sat next to her on the couch playing video games and eating popcorn.

"Hey, it's for an article I'm doing," Alex said through a mouthful of kernels when Mittens complained. "It's research."

For the hundredth time, Mittens read the letter Ruffled Feathers sent Roland. It didn't tell her anything new.

Finally, she tucked it into her folder. "I wonder if we'll run into Ruffled Feathers again. That had to be him at the Yodeling Toad."

"I wonder why he targeted Grandma Basset," Alex said.

"I wonder if he'll do it again."

Alex put an arm around his partner's shoulders, spilling his popcorn all over her skirt. "If he does, we'll be ready for him."

Mittens scooped up a handful of kernels. "Count on it, partner."

devotional

Theme Verse

Dear friends, never take revenge.
Leave that to the righteous anger of
God. For the Scriptures say,
  "I will take revenge;
    I will pay them back,"
    says the Lord.

Romans 12:19

Food for Thought

Robert Roland was a good worker—at first. He did honest work at the Tasty Treats factory. He was a trusted member of Grandma Basset's team, and his flavors brought smiles to many customers... especially Alex!

But then he started to feel under appreciated. That's when the trouble started.

What did Robert Roland do to get back at Grandma Basset?

Because Robert was hurting, he wanted to hurt Grandma back. So he stole her recipe to ruin her big day.

This type of behavior is called revenge. It's an easy sin to fall into.

At first, revenge sounds like a great way to make yourself feel better when someone wrongs you. After all, how many times do we see this theme in a superhero or action movie?

Can you think of a time when you felt wronged? What did you do? How did you feel after?

Getting revenge will never make you feel better because such behavior is not part of God's plan for our lives.

Romans 12:9 says, "Beloved, never avenge yourselves, but leave it to the wrath of God. For it is written, 'Vengeance is mine, I will repay,' says the Lord."

God wants us to trust Him to make things right when people hurt us.

Now, we should still be honest about how we feel! God wants us to communicate with each other openly. You can't have a relationship with someone if you are hiding the truth from them.

The problem is, it's scary to be vulnerable. Telling someone how they hurt you takes a lot of courage.

Instead of stealing, what could Robert have done to help Grandma Basset understand he felt ignored? How do you think she would have responded?

Lying, stealing, taking things into our own hands instead of trusting God...these are all sins.

A long time ago, Jesus died for the sins of God's people. If you're a Christian, that means He died for you, too! Because of Jesus, God has forgiven your sins and welcomed you into His family for eternity. That's wonderful news!

Our actions still have consequences, however. Even though Grandma Basset forgave Robert—and brought him back onto her team—he still had to live with the consequences of his sin by performing community service.

Think of a moment you did something wrong. Your parents probably forgave you, but there might have been a consequence

for your behavior. Talk about this moment.
What do you think your parents are trying
to teach you?

The next time somebody wrongs you, think about the lesson Robert Roland learned. How can you make a wrong situation right without taking revenge?

alex's glossary

Hi kids!

Hope you enjoyed our first mystery!

Let's be honest: I don't always understand every word Mittens says. Do you?

When that happens, I have to use Google to look up their definitions. I thought I'd save you some time by sneaking my notes into the back of the book.

Hope it helps!

Alex

———

Chapter 1

Bicentennial: Two hundred.

Ceremony: An event that celebrates something special. Often, someone gives a speech and there is food.

Cowering: To be very afraid.

Culinary: Related to cooking.

Elaborate: Fancy, highly decorated, or complex.

Foremost: Best, top, or strongest.

Graffiti: Putting paint, writing, stickers, or other markings on the side of a building without permission. This behavior can get you into trouble with the law.

Inside story: An article on the inside of a newspaper.

Investigative reporters: Journalists who specialize in uncovering the truth, especially in situations where other people try to hide the truth. Like detectives!

Relatively: Close but not exact.

Underestimate: To think too little of.

Warbled: To go in or out, or to get loud and then quiet. Uneven and inconsistent.

Chapter 2

Combination: Several things together. Or, in the case of a safe, the series of numbers that unlocks the safe.

Designated: To be set aside for something specifically.

Engineer: Someone with a lot of education who is good at planning, building, or creating things.

Insensitive: Rude or unkind.

Marketing: The act of telling people about an item or service you sell and convincing them to buy it.

Mechanism: The parts of something that make it work. Could be gears, pulleys, belts, circuit boards, switches, wheels, or other elements.

Prime suspects: The suspects who most likely committed a crime.

Chapter 3

Autograph: To sign something with your name.

Baseboard: A narrow board running along the base of a room's wall.

Clues: Things detectives use to help them decide who committed a crime. This can be physical evidence like fingerprints or a torn piece of clothing. It can also be odd pieces of behavior, lies, or strange comments.

Concentrate: To focus hard on something.

Desperate: To need something so badly, you do things you wouldn't normally do.

Perimeter: The edge of something.

Priority: Something you decide is more important than something else.

Unreasonable: To be irrational, illogical. To believe something without good reason.

Chapter 4

Corporate: A large company that has multiple departments, lots of workers, and one group of leaders responsible for making decisions.

Depart: To leave.

Disturb: To interfere with the normal routine. To bother.

Lemongrass: A plant often used to help treat medical conditions, like stomachaches, fevers, and colds.

Organic: Grown without the use of artificial fertilizers, bug-treatments, or ingredients.

Overwhelm: To surround, cover up, or fill so completely, it is difficult to sense anything other than the thing that is overwhelming.

Precise: Neat, careful, and without error.

Resigned: To quit or give up.

Restrained: Held back or tied down.

Straitjacket: A type of jacket that pins your arms to your sides. This is used in medical situations where the patient is out of control.

Chapter 5

Interview: To talk with someone for the purpose of learning information they have.

Lederhosen: An old-fashioned type of shorts with H-shaped suspenders, traditionally worn by people living in the area around the Alps, such as Bavaria, Germany, and Switzerland.

Pudgy: Short and chubby.

Suspenders: Elastic straps that clip onto the front and back of a pair of pants. They go over the shoulders and help keep the pants in place.

Yodel: A type of singing originating from the German/Swiss/Bavarian regions. The singer rapidly changes between very high notes and low notes.

Chapter 6

Confectionary: A place that sells candy, chocolate, and other sweets.

Conspiracy: A secret plan made by a secret group to do something bad or to hide the truth about something.

Contributing: Adding to. Helping.

Drawl: A slow, gentle way of speaking.

Enthusiastic: Excited, loud, eager, and happy.

Illuminated: To light up a space with a light source.

Memorized: To look at something and recite it until you can recall it from memory without looking at the original source.

Patrons: People who shop at a store or eat at a restaurant.

Silhouette: The basic outline of someone's shape without any specific details. Like a shadow.

Succession: When something happens in a row, one right after another.

Superior: The best.

Temples: When describing parts of the body, this word refers to the sides of your face. It's the space above your ears but below your hair, close to your eyes.

VIP: An abbreviation that means "Very Important Person."

Chapter 7

Community service: A type of punishment where you serve a certain number of hours doing something helpful for the community to make up for a small crime. For example: Picking up trash, painting a building, or planting flowers at the park.

Hypnotic: Easy to stare at, hard to look away from.

become a
bowwow barker

Greetings, readers!

Alex and Mittens here. Listen, we've been thinking...

This is a big world. There are a lot of questions that need to be answered. And plenty of truth that needs to be discovered.

We want your help! If you like:

- Reading
- Asking big questions
- Searching for clues
- Finding God's truth hidden in the world

...then boy, do we have a club for you.

Join our league of junior detectives: the **Bowwow Barkers**!

As a Bowwow Barker, you'll get occasional emails from Mittens. (And Alex, if he remembers to send them.)

We'll teach you how to be junior detectives through a series of activities you can do at home.

And you'll be the first to know when a new Collar Cases book is available. You'll also receive invitations to free Barkers-only events, like virtual educational activities or in-person parties.

We may even send you snacks!

Hold on...

Never mind. Mittens just said the post office doesn't let us do that. But maybe we'll send you other fun goodies.

The best news? It's free to join!

To sign up:

- Have an adult go to www.CollarCases.com

- Scroll down to the big "Join the Club!" Button
- Click!

If you get busy, you can always unsubscribe and rejoin us later. No hard feelings!

Until next time, keep your pencils sharp, turn in your homework on time, and watch out for aliens.

All our best,

Mittens & Alex

find more collar cases

The mystery continues in *Collar Cases #2: Case of the Missing Monet!*

It's a quiet day in Bowwow when Alex helps Mittens take her nieces to the local art museum for a day of hands-on learning. But then a valuable painting is stolen from a new exhibit!

Can Mittens and Alex recover the painting before it's lost forever?

Is this another crime organized by the mysterious Ruffled Feathers?

More importantly, can the inhabitants of

Bowwow survive the antics of the rambunctious Kastle kittens?

Find out in *Collar Cases #2: Case of the Missing Monet*. Available now in paperback, audiobook, and ebook.

Audiobook: Mittens and Alex talk!

Take your reading experience to the next level with our fully-voiced audiobooks. Available for each title.

Every Collar Cases character comes to life with distinct voices, made possible by the terrific narration of Trista Shaye, author of over 100 audiobooks.

This format is the perfect choice for family road trips!

Ebook: Creator commentary!

Learn more about the illustration process with the **Illustrator's Commentary** (ebook exclusive).

Each image contains a brief note from

illustrator Sarah Johnson discussing artistic technique, her reasons behind composition decisions, and advice to young artists.

If you're an aspiring author, check out the **Advice for Young Writers** column, also exclusive to ebook. This short letter from the author teaches young writers an element of the craft or process.

————

No matter what format you choose, we hope Collar Cases brings your family hours of clean, Bible-based fun!

author lady

Amanda Trumpower writes for Jesus lovers who dig dragons, detectives, and droids. She's a twin mom, second-generation homeschooler, D&D enthusiast, and board game fanatic.

She's been writing ever since she could hold a crayon, but really cranked up the WPM after upgrading to a keyboard.

Learn more at AmandaTrumpower.com.

illustrator lady

Sarah Johnson's story-based illustrations compose playful worlds for the young at heart.

When she's not scrutinizing colors, Sarah enjoys learning new board games, crocheting, and spoiling her cats, Wanda & Pietro.

narrator lady

Trista Shaye is a lively, vivid narrator who specializes in fully-voiced readings—meaning she will bring each character to life with unique voices.

The award-winning narrator has voiced over 100 audiobooks of various genres, is the voice of several characters in audio-drama podcasts, and has even recorded an advertisement for LEGO.

Trista is also an author who writes for middle grade and YA audiences. All of her books are clean and enjoyable for the entire family. She also writes and directs *Tales of Ezmeer,* an epic fantasy podcast.

Made in the USA
Middletown, DE
17 February 2022

61239110R00057